In the Devils Arms

By: Ashlyn Bragg

To the dreamers in the Universe

Chapter 1

Mike

I sighed as I continued to look through the thick file folder my father had brought to my office. I knew exactly what I would find when I finally decided to look through it, but it wasn't like it was something I had planned on dealing with this young. I'm a twenty-two year old made man in my fathers' business. Or as he likes to call it, the Cusumano Family. He's old school though and believes that every good Italian man should be put into an advantageous marriage. And by advantageous he means that I must marry an Italian woman of his selection. A woman that both he and my mother, God rest her soul, would approve of in every way.

Now the old man would like to say that he has complete control over just whom I end up married to, but he also realizes that times have changed. He wants me to marry a woman that I can be faithful to, to provide him with grandchildren and further heirs to the family business, or better put a woman that I won't turn away the first time I lay my eyes on her. Pop claims that he wants me to have a marriage like he and my mothers, which is all good and well. I mean, Pop never once raised a hand to my mother, nor did he step out on her with any of the women working in any of our clubs. Their marriage was one that I respected and looked up to. It wasn't always sunshine and roses, but hell what marriage honestly is.

But I needed to focus. Pop expected me to narrow this file down to my top five before the end of business today. I pinched my nose as I thumbed through the folder again. Pictures taken from different distances and vantage points throughout the city flipped slowly in a kaleidoscope of colors. Figures he'd have our men out snapping pictures of 'suitable' Italian women all for me. He knew that I'd been with several ladies over the years since I'd been made, but none of them were proper enough. Quite a few of them worked in our various clubs. It wasn't like I had a type. I'm still young enough to like going out and having a taste here and there.

A few faces jumped out at me, and I knew that there was more information provided for me to get to know a little about each woman. What surprised me most was as I read through the information on several of the women was that either one or both of their parents owed a significant debt to our family. I should have known that he was going to take advantage of someone else's situation. He wouldn't want to have some father refusing to marry his daughter to a guy like me.

The Cusumano Family wasn't exactly known for being all good guys. We're still a part of the mafia even though most of our businesses have been turning legit over the past fifteen years. Pop started turning things around after we had a few major losses. He lost several men, my baby sister Alessia was almost kidnapped, and I became a made man protecting her. And we lost my mother.

***

A rival family decided to make a go at taking out me as my fathers' heir when I was twelve. On a regular outing with two year old Alessia, her nanny, and a few guards, the Parisi family made their move while we were making our way through the local park. It was a beautiful day out when several Parisi goons jumped out of a car parked along the edge of the park. Guns drawn, they fired at us and our guards. One stray bullet managed to hit the nanny and she went down as someone made a grab for Alessia.

I did the only thing that I could think to do in order to do what I knew my father would want. Grabbing one of our downed guards' guns, I turned and squeezed the trigger on a man reaching into my sisters' stroller. As another man began to make his way toward us, I pulled off another shot. I watched as two of our enemies fell trying to snatch my baby sister. I watched the blood oozing from their chest wounds, both of my shots had hit center mass. I watched as the life drained from their faces and they bled out in the park. After tucking the gun into the back waste of my pants, I reached into the stroller for Alessia and began to soothe her the way her nanny had. Someone must have made a call during all the chaos; sirens were roaring all around and cops were beginning to show up. But so were more of Pops' men. They were about to move in to sweep Alessia and myself up.

Only they stopped. They allowed the cops to come to us first, allowing for proper reports to be made. It was obvious that this was just mob violence that was getting out of hand and the only ones left standing in that moment were two children. Pop would allow the cops to take their reports while ensuring that the only thing I went down for was killing the two men in self-defense. It was obvious that I was only doing what I could to protect myself and my baby sister. Then I would report to my father everything that had happened, and revenge would be served up to the one family that had had the balls to make such a move. Pop would make sure that the Parisi's paid for their insolence. And if there was one thing I knew, even at twelve years of age, no one brought vengeance like Leonardo Cusumano.

***

I honestly wasn't sure how to take it that Pop wants me married to the daughter of someone that owes him so much money. There had to be a reason behind it all. He would probably forgive their debt, but would he allow them to become indebted to him again? And if he did, how would he get them to forgive them once more? It wasn't like he had that many kids to marry off. I didn't see him giving Alessia away as a bride to just anyone.

Flipping through more pictures, I suddenly stopped as one caught my attention. I'd never once been so completely drawn to a woman the way that I was to her. Any other woman, I could take her once maybe twice if she was particularly pleasing, and then set her loose to take care of some other guy. But this one, she was stunning. A breath of fresh air to the darkness that flooded my soul daily. Blonde hair that flowed freely to the center of her back and dark eyes that looked troubled. I had to know who she was. This one. She was the woman I would tell my father to introduce me to. If I had anything to say about it, she would be mine tonight without a marriage certificate in place.

Her information wasn't too terribly detailed, but I could tell exactly why she had been added to this file. Carina Romano had had plans to attend one of the most prestigious colleges in town, but now she was stuck waiting tables at a local mom and pop diner. Her parents had lost her entire college fund in one of our family's casinos. Of course, the Romanos' would happily put their only daughter up as the bride of their biggest debt. Pop would already have plans in place to start getting our money back from them if I chose anyone other than Carina. And the look in her eyes said she would do anything to take care of her parents, even if they were the ones that had fucked her over.

I couldn't allow that to happen. I couldn't let this Angel believe that she would always be responsible for her parents' debts. This would end her ties to them in every way. I would ensure that with Pop before the contracts were even drawn up. Once my Angel was mine, they would have no ties to her. She would no longer answer to them, and she would be a Cusumano in every way.

Chapter 2

Carina

It was time to get ready for yet another day of waiting on people at Salvador's, a locally owned diner that most of the teens frequented. It also saw its' own fair share of families in the later hours of the evening and those getting off from second shift in the factories. I'd been working there with my mom ever since I'd been old enough to get a job with dreams of leaving home once I'd graduated high school. Thankfully, Sal the owner, never put us on the same shifts. He was a smart man and knew that mama would weasel her way to taking my nights tips every time.

I still couldn't believe that my parents could be so completely selfish. They used every dollar from my inheritance that had been set aside for college to gamble in one of the Cusumano casinos on the shore. Mama had said they had a sure thing going at the tables one night and they'd been on the ups when suddenly their luck had turned. Didn't they realize that the house always won? Didn't they realize that they were ruining my one shot at a better life than repeating their mistakes? Of course not. They had been incredibly greedy then and still were now.

"Carina! Come down here, we have much to discuss." My father called for me from downstairs. When he said things in that tone, I knew instantly that there was going to be trouble. And usually, it ended up with me having to do something to get them out of that trouble.

It wasn't bad enough that I am working as a waitress in the same diner that my mother has worked in for years. She'd bucked against her own parents' wishes when she was younger in order to marry my father and been cut off as a result. However, as their only grandchild, her parents had done what they could to make sure I had a leg up. They'd set up an inheritance for me to use for college. My parents weren't even supposed to have access to it, but papers had been placed in front of me and I had been in such a rush to get to a summer class one morning that I hadn't read it. I'd inadvertently signed away my college money to them to feed their gambling habits. And they'd once more left me high and dry.

Straightening up my uniforms skirt, I took a moment longer to look over myself once more in the full length mirror in my childhood bedroom. I couldn't even afford to move out of my parents' home now that they'd taken all my money. My one escape from this place. I was just lucky enough that they hadn't decided to charge me rent to continue living under their roof now that I was nineteen years old. I attempted a smile at my reflection as I gave one more tug at my high ponytail.

"Carina! Did you not hear your father? I swear… that girl…" mom began to holler. As if I couldn't hear the muttering that followed her calling for me once more.

"Coming." I called, scooping up a light sweater and my purse on the way out of my bedroom. If I could just scrape enough money together for rent, I'd leave this house. I had to find some way to get out from underneath their thumbs or else I wasn't going to make it. They were killing my spirit in ways I'd never thought possible.

The moment I stepped off the last step, I could hear the words slipping easily off my mother's lips. "Finally! I swear, if we had the money, we'd get your ears checked Carina." It figures that my mother would bring up money issues so flippantly. If we had the money to get my ears checked, they wouldn't be spending it on an ear doctors appointment.

Of course, if we had the money, they wouldn't spend a dime on me. I knew that just as well as they did. Anytime they had money, they'd turn around and lose it at the casino once more. They were always in debt to the Cusumano family. It wouldn't surprise me if they were about to tell me they needed money again. Money that I didn't have to give them. I was saving up, but I refused to tell them that.

My parents were sitting in the living room which hadn't changed since my early childhood. We still had the same old furniture that we'd had for years. The walls were covered with old family pictures, but very few included me for some reason. It was like the only reason I existed to my parents was the tax break they received yearly on their taxes. And last year had been the final year they'd been able to really claim that. It was apparent that I was more burden than treasure for them, always had been. Hopefully, I'd be able to relieve them of being such a burden sooner rather than later.

"Sit. Sit. We have wonderful news for you, Carina." Dad had a slimy grin forming on his face and it gave me the feeling that this wonderful news wasn't going to be good for me at all. But I did as I was instructed because it was easier to just comply for the time being. The sooner dad got this out of his system, the sooner I could begin to make my way to work. "We've chosen the perfect husband for you, Carina." He stated as if I should be honored by the declaration.

I had to have misheard him. "I'm sorry, but… what?" I asked, stumped. There was no way I would marry a total stranger. Hell, I didn't have time to date let alone get to know someone and plan a wedding. No way could this happen. And I wasn't the type to marry just because he was good looking or had a lot of money. I wasn't ready for that kind of commitment. Who was at my age?

No way would my parents just marry me off to anyone. I mean okay yeah; it'd get me out of their house and probably help lower some of their bills. But who would keep them going to work so that they could pay those bills? Wait! When did I become the parent in this situation? I continued to stare at my father, his button down shirt open over a slightly stained white undershirt. "You heard me right, Carina. You're getting married. And if he has anything to say about it, the sooner the better." He stated, rubbing his hands together greedily. I could smell a rat or two, and I was currently looking at both. Something was up and they were going to profit from this marriage.

Married? And soon? Nothing was making sense as my mother placed a glass in front of me. "You're looking a little flush, Carina. Have something to drink before you think about fainting." She ordered me. Since when was mom concerned on whether I fainted or not. I hadn't done it in the past, but this was big news. This was life altering in every way. And from the way dad was putting it, I wouldn't have a say in the matter. But they would profit from it. I knew they would. Selling their only child for financial gain.

I reached for the glass without a second thought and downed it in one long swallow. My parents watched me closely as I did. My skin began to crawl as I realized I'd probably done something that was not in my best interests. The drink seemed fine really, just some apple juice which my mother knew I loved having at least a glass of every day. Then, suddenly the room began to move. Dad took the glass away from me before I could drop it as I gripped the back of the couch. I tried to stand, my legs shaky and both of my parents moving to follow me. It was obvious that they weren't going to let me out of their sight. "What did you do?" I asked, my words beginning to slur as my vision started swimming.

"It's best for everyone, Carina." Mom said. She and dad reached out to keep me steady. My legs were starting to shake as I tried to continue standing. Suddenly, they were completely supporting my weight as the room around me went completely black. "Best for us, really." She murmured as I lost consciousness. Not that I knew what she meant. I wouldn't find out until later, and that seemed to be what both my mother and father were aiming for.

Chapter 3

She was unconscious when she'd been delivered to our estate by her parents, and I was immediately furious. This was not how I'd agreed for this to all go down. I wanted to meet Carina like any other guy, preferably in a public place so that she would feel somewhat safe meeting her future husband. I could've ended Ernesto and Constance Romano's worthless lives then and there. It certainly would have cost our family a hell of a lot less money to just put the older couple out of their misery. And it probably wouldn't have hurt Carina either. Thankfully, they hadn't just dumped her out on the front stoop and waited with hands out to take the check my father was writing them. Debt forgiven and all, but the check was my stipulation to my father. He would pay them off, force them to leave our town and never look back. With the way they'd brought Carina to us, it was obvious they weren't hurt in the least by losing their only daughter. Even I would show her more respect than that.

One of our men had been the one to carry her inside, bringing her into the living room and laying her carefully on the couch as I glowered at the Romanos'. I'd deal with Giacomo later for even daring to put his hands on my fiancé. No other man would ever touch her again. Her soft skin was mine to touch and tease, and mine alone. I'd never reacted like this before. There was something about Carina that set her apart from the numerous other women I'd taken to bed. As our parents stepped into my fathers' office without a backwards glance towards myself or Carina, I moved to get a better look at my own personal angel. "Leave us." I muttered to Giacomo. I didn't want him even witnessing this partial introduction. The first person that I wanted my Carina to lay eyes on once she came around was me. "Wait… Giacomo, fetch the doctor. I want to make sure that her parents haven't brought me a bride on her death bed." He nodded as he stepped from the living room to make the appropriate phone calls.

As I took a seat on the coffee table across from her, I reached out to gently brush a longish strand of that blond hair away from her face. More than anything, I wanted this beautiful angel to open her eyes. I wanted her to look at me as I looked at her. And I wanted to make her mine. Immediately! But I couldn't do any of that while she was unconscious. I refused to take from her as her own parents had done. I would give her the world. She would no longer have to wear this ridiculous waitress outfit, with the high ponytail. No, my bride would be able to go to her university. She would have the education that she craved and had quite frankly earned.

The office door opened easily, and I sat up a little straighter on the coffee table without taking my eyes off my angel. The conversation between her parents and my father was quiet, probably trying to keep the *kids* from knowing as much as possible. It wouldn't matter though; Carina was still unconscious and hadn't moved once since Giacomo had laid her down on the couch. And dad would discuss anything I needed to know about later. I knew that the business would be quickly conducted and that neither of us would be required to sign anything at this time. No, our signatures would come next week when we signed our marriage license. Her parents had been told correctly. I would marry her as soon as humanly possible.

The Romanos' were escorted out through the front door just as Doctor Mascolo was brought in through a side door. Giacomo was very good about keeping things discreet and there was no way that I wanted Carinas' parents to know that I was having her checked over.

"Can we move her to somewhere the young miss will perhaps be more comfortable?" Doc asked.

I didn't think anything of it as I stood quickly and easily scooped her small body up into my arms. She practically weighed nothing and felt so right in my arms. And yet, even as I moved her slightly to get the best hold on her body, Carina didn't move once or make a sound. It worried me still and I led the way quickly upstairs to my bedroom. It was luxuriously decorated in bold blues and shades of cream that brought images of the ocean to mind. Doc nodded towards the bed, and I moved over to lay her on top of the comforter. Once she'd been checked over thoroughly by the family doctor, I'd get her more comfortable myself.

"You can leave us, Michael. Your woman is safe with me." He assured me. And since I'd known this man for years, hell he'd delivered me and Alessia in this very house, I stepped outside. The door was still cracked, just in case my angel should begin to stir.

***

It was an agonizing hour before Doc finally came back out of my room and eased the door almost completely shut. I could still see her body laid out on my bed just as I'd left her earlier, and I could tell that she hadn't moved much if at all. "Anything, Doc?" I asked, my voice low as I began to crack my knuckles. If they poisoned her, harmed her in any way before they'd brought her to my family estate, I would hunt the Romanos' down and end them.

"She seems to be fine. Resting comfortably." The older male held up a smaller cooler with what I could only assume would be blood vials. "I drew blood to be on the safe side, but Miss. Carina appears to only be sleeping. If I had to guess, I'd think that her parents drugged her to ensure she got here without a fight. But I will be able to tell you more in a few days."

"When will she wake up?"

Doc gave a small shrug as we began to walk down the main staircase. He had seen worse with this family. Maybe even far worse than he used to see when he'd worked in the county's' emergency room. "It could be a few hours or possibly tomorrow at the latest. Michael, if it was a sleeping medication that she was given, it all depends on the dosage she was given. But I don't feel like your Miss. Carina is in any real danger. Her vitals are stable, and she does not appear to be in any form of discomfort. If I were you, I'd keep a close eye on her throughout the night. If anything should change, I'm only a phone call away." And I knew he said that because we wouldn't call 911. We never had, not even in the direst of situations because calling that number ended up with police reports. The Cusumano's did not want to deal with the cops ever. We'd go to jail before making any statements.

I walked Doc out to his Mercedes, holding the driver's door open as he eased behind the steering wheel. "We'll call if there are any problems. But I'll also send one of my men to pick you up." Doc was getting up there in age and I knew that he didn't like driving in the dark. There was no way that I'd risk the life of the one man that could help my Carina. Shutting his door, I stepped back and watched as he pulled out of our driveway. Time to return to my fiancé.

Chapter 4

Carina

I stifled a groan as I began to awaken. My head was absolutely pounding, and I had no idea when or where I was. The last thing that I remembered was drinking that glass of apple juice my mother had given me. Obviously, she'd slipped me something and I was just now coming out of its affects. First thing I needed to do was get myself upright. I needed to figure out what had happened since I'd been unconscious and then find my mother. I needed… no wanted to know what exactly had been going through her mind. What mother in their right mind drugs their own daughter? But first, I needed to find some aspirin for this splitting headache.

Something was off though as I pulled one hand out from underneath the silky sheets. They didn't feel like the older t-shirt material that I had become accustomed to over the years. No, these sheets had an expensive feeling to them. They were softer and silkier than anything I'd ever felt in my life. Whatever this material was wrapped around my body, I liked it. And for once in my life, not knowing where I was or how I'd gotten here, I felt safe. This room had a clean scent to it, not that my room didn't smell clean. It was a different kind of clean and not one that I was put off by. This was just more… masculine. My hand continued its upwards trajectory towards my head, feeling the shirt I was wearing. Whatever I was wearing was far more expensive than the cheap polyester material of my waitressing uniform. Now I was beginning to freak out.

Opening one eye, I groaned as the pain in my head rose. I looked to the window and noticed that the curtains were open, and a gentle breeze was blowing into the room. From the sunlight streaming in, I realized that I had been out for hours. It was already tomorrow, and I'd missed a full day of work. Wonder if mom even bothered to call our boss and make up an excuse as to why I suddenly couldn't come in. Or had she even bothered? Would I have a job when I made it in for my next shift or I would I be outright fired? I was really starting to freak out the more I took in of where I was. And I still had no clue as to my where I was. Then my eyes landed on him.

I tried not to freak out as my eyes slowly took in his half-nakedness. Long legs covered in black slacks and a white dress shirt completely unbuttoned. The sunlight was carefully dancing against along every exposed inch of golden tanned skin. I noticed a design tattooed into the skin of his side, climbing his rib cage as he took in a slow breath. It was obvious to me that he was still peacefully sleeping. What amazed me from taking in his position was that it didn't seem like he'd tried to take advantage of me. I wasn't feeling any kind of soreness or stiffness throughout my body. He could have done anything to me in my state, but I don't think he did. So far, I have no evidence to prove that thought wrong.

As I began to move around, slowly pushing into a seated position, I tried to be as quiet as possible. Just because it seemed like he hadn't attempted anything the night before, I still had no idea who this man was. I tried to look around the room, taking in the differing shades of blues and creams. It was masculine while giving off an ocean vibe. And it was calming. Surprising, yet calming. But my eyes couldn't stray away from the man for very long. I know that there is no way he'll sleep all day. He'll probably awaken sooner rather than later, and I really need to stop staring at him. Or more precisely at his abs. Just as I'm pushing back the covers, his phone starts to go off, and I'm pulling the covers up all the way to my chin.

I'm not scared per say, but I don't know this guy. He could be a killer for all I know. He could have other plans of what he wants to do to me, and all he was waiting for was me to be awake. And now, I'm awake. He jerked awake and rubbing a hand over his face, blindly grabbed his phone from the nightstand.

"Yeah?" he asked to whomever was on the other end. I couldn't hear the person on the other side, but it was obvious when blue eyes turned to me that I was the topic of conversation. "Looks like she's awake. I will let you know the status as soon as I know." Without another word, he ended the call and focused completely on me. He took his time in looking me over or at least what he could see of me. I swear that I'm not hiding, but a grin still slowly formed on his lips as he stood up and gave a stretch. My eyes once again followed the lines of his torso, moving upwards until our eyes met once more. His grin seemed a little cockier as he took in the look on my face, took in the way that I bit down into my bottom lip.

"How are you feeling?" His question surprised me, but I knew that he was being sincere. As I tried to push myself up into more of a sitting position in the bed, he moved to help me. "Take it easy. Apparently, whatever your parents gave you last night was some pretty strong shit." I don't think I want to know how he knows what my parents put in my drink. Was he involved in all of this? I cleared my throat softly, trying to form the words to find out how bad this was all going to end up being for me. Could I honestly trust this guy that I didn't even have a name for.

"Where am I?" I asked, my voice coming out a little scratchy even for the early morning hours. I reached up to rub gingerly at my throat as the man instantly moved over to a table across the room. He poured me a glass of what appeared to be ice water. I still wasn't sure, and he could see it in my eyes. I motioned between the two of us and I had to ask. "Did we?"

He looked appalled as he roughly shook his head. "I would never take advantage of a woman who was in your condition last night, nor would I ever force myself on an unwilling woman, Carina." He stated emphatically. So emphatically that I believed him. This man that somehow knew my name, yet I still didn't know his, looked like he could be physically ill by the thought alone. A part of me felt safer knowing that, but still I was in an unfamiliar place in what had to be this guys bed. And I was no longer in my own clothes. "Yes, I had a little help getting you into something you might be a little more comfortable sleeping in, but I promise I didn't peak. One of the maids… she helped with that part…" he mumbled.

He moved to help me sit up further and held the glass out to me. "It's just water." He told me, sitting down beside me on the edge of the bed. He never once made a move to pull the covers off me or push me into anything. "As for where you are, you're at my family's estate." My eyebrow quirked at that statement, and he once again smiled at me. This time it was more of a genuine smile than the earlier cocky grins. It was like he was proud of who his family was and where he came from. "We're outside of the city. When you're feeling up to it, I'll take you out for a little tour of the grounds. You'll want to know more about your new home and how to get around this place if I'm working."

My new home? I wanted to scream and kick at that thought. And then I remembered last nights conversation my father had barely started before I'd drank my juice. I finally took the glass of water from this stranger and looked at him in question. It was obvious that he was the only one in the room that knew exactly what was going on. Taking a slow sip, the cool water felt good as I swallowed, and it helped in soothing my scratchy throat. "What makes you think this is my new home?"

"We're getting married." He began, watching me closely once more for a response. "Next week."

Chapter 5

Mike

It's been over a week since my Carina came to live at our estate. She argues with me daily on the wedding, refusing to do any kind of planning towards it. It's like she doesn't see the advantages she will have once we are married. I've already told her that she will no longer have to worry about her parents. Their debt with my family was cleared the moment they'd signed the marriage agreement. Then my father had *generously* given them enough money for a fresh start far away from their daughter. We already knew with how easily the agreement had been reached that they seemed to care little for Carina. It was even further nailed home with the way they'd carelessly drugged her to get her to the estate.

Thankfully, the sleeping drugs they'd selected had only been strong enough to knock her out for several hours. After she'd awakened, I'd had Doc come back out and give her another once over just to make sure there would be no lasting effects. Doc had me step out of the room so that he could go over a few things privately with Carina. As much as I had wanted to be privy to everything about my future wife, I understood that there were things that she needed to figure out on her own.

Carina and I had been taking the past week to get to know a little bit about one another. We'd take long walks throughout the estate grounds. I'd tell her where we were, and she'd tell me a little of what she wanted out of life. And we would continue these conversations until she knew every inch of the Cusumano estate. But I'd yet to make a move on her. She was mine and I hadn't even kissed her. She didn't know too much about the family or at least I hadn't told her anything. It wasn't like she couldn't do her own research though, and I was certain by now she had. She had plenty of downtime when I wasn't with her to do so.

Stepping into the breakfast nook, I nodded at our cook as she began working on my first coffee of the morning. Carina was already dressed in a frilly summer dress that I'd purchased for her and looking over a course book for college. Her parents blowing through her college fund may have stopped her from starting school this semester, but one of the first things I'd promised her one our first day together was that she would be able to get the education that she wanted for herself. I would pay for it, and she could start at the beginning of next semester. Her face lit up immediately, and it pleased me to be able to put that look on her face. Then I had to remind her, our wedding would come first.

I wasn't looking for a big, flashy wedding. The press would be given access for just the right number of pictures to publish. Obviously, the fact that Michael Cusumano is getting married will be big news. I've never hidden the fact that I'm not the marrying type. I wouldn't have started now except for the fact that I am getting married. Carina Romano is a very lucky woman in being able to saddle me down to only one woman. Or at least that's how the press will put it.

Leaning over Carina, I pressed a quick kiss to the top of her head. She barely paid attention to it, her attention still fully pouring into the coursebook in front of her. "Good morning, Angel." I murmured softly for her ears only as I pulled my phone from my coats inside pocket. I pulled up my calendar app and put the phone down where she could see it. "Either we set a date for the wedding now, or I will take you to the courthouse for a ceremony with a judge." And she knew I meant it. I made no bones about how I felt towards this wedding happening. It could be as big or small as she wanted, but she had to start making inroads with planning.

"Whichever works for me, Mike." She replied with a shrug, taking a sip of her own coffee. She highlighted a class she seemed interested in before I could pull the book away from her. "Mike…" Carina finally looked up at me and our eyes met. I smirked as I leaned in closer to her. I left barely an inch between our lips, breathing in her sweet floral scent as I continued to stare into her eyes. Her tongue flicked out to wet her bottom lip, gently brushing against my own, and drawing another grin from me. "May I please have my book back?"

"Pick a date." Honestly, it was simple. I had something she wanted, she had an answer I wanted. A little of give and take seemed to make this relationship flourish. She sighed as she leaned back, snatching up my phone from the tabletop and glancing at the empty dates on my calendar. I had no worry of what she might find in my schedule because everything was coded. It had to be in this life. I couldn't have an execution or payment pickup marked as what they were. But I watched her all the same, taking in the way she studied each date before her. It wasn't like she had much to do until the next semester started anyway. I hated to think that, but it was true.

Unless I put a baby in her belly immediately. I hadn't made it a secret in the least that our marriage would be real in every way. I would have her in every sense of the word. Carina knew that she would be mine and only made a few simple requests. No cheating whatsoever. Easy enough, she knew that I wanted the kind of marriage that my parents had. Or at least the public perception of it. I wouldn't step out on her and it was a promise I could make without regret. Her second request was a little harder, but I finally agreed with a little give on her end. She wanted sex to wait until after everything was legal. I said that was going to be a little hard on my end and that she had to give me a little something or I was lucky to go find someone who was more than willing to give it up until the wedding. Carina hadn't liked that in the least and we worked out a compromise.

I could touch her if I stopped when she said to. "I'm not going to take advantage of you, Carina. Yes, you are a beautiful woman. But I'm not the guy that's going to do something you're not willing to do it. I won't force you." I had promised her solemnly. And I was a man of my word. No matter how long she made me wait for this wedding to happen, we both know that it will happen. We both know that the wedding night is fast coming, and on that night, I will have her.

I reached underneath the table with one hand, taking a sip of my coffee as I lightly gripped her thigh. My touch was gentle, but firm enough to garner her attention as I gave a short squeeze and then teasingly ran my fingers along her inner thigh. Watching her closely, I caught the way she bit into her bottom lip, her eyes flashing over to me as the cook brought over breakfast for both of us. I knew I wouldn't push it any further, my fingers never once even dipping up underneath the hemline of her dress, but I wanted her to know that I could until she told me to stop. "Fine. Here!" she said, dropping my phone in front of me after selecting a date. It was obvious that I was getting to her. I seemed to have a way of pushing her buttons in a way that soon she would give me what I wanted.

Without taking my eyes off her, I grinned in triumph. "Shall I call the judge and make an appointment?" I asked. She nodded her head as she picked up her spoon. "You sure you don't want a big church wedding?" It was something that I'd asked her several times over this past week. And everything I received the same answer. There would be no one to sit on the brides side of any church we might have selected, and she honestly hadn't ever really wanted a large wedding. It seemed that both Carina and I could both be happy with something that was small and much more intimate. Finally, I pulled my gaze away from her and looked down at my phone and gave a short laugh. "Guess I will be calling the judge, as well as calling in a few favors." From her confused look, I turned my phone for her to see the date she'd selected.

"Fuck…" she stated, laying her forehead in her palms. I didn't think she'd been paying attention to the screen when she'd pushed the date. Her focus had been on my hand that was still resting on her thigh. I pulled back and purposely marked the date for our nuptials.

"Too late now, Angel. Tomorrow afternoon, you're going to become Mrs. Michael Cusumano." I told her, already dialing the first contact I needed to get this ball rolling. I stood up without touching my breakfast, pressing another kiss to the top of her forehead. "Feel free to call up one or two of my cousins to help you find a dress and whatever else you're gonna need. And take Giacomo with you if you have to leave the house." Carina didn't even get a chance to hiccup as I made my way out of the kitchen. This wedding was on the fast track, and I needed to get my side of the planning done quickly. "Pop…" I said into the phone as I made my way out of the house.

Chapter 6

Carina

I can't believe that I fell for all of that yesterday. Go figure that Mike would use the simmering attraction we shared for one another already against me. He knew that I wanted to get everything as far as school was concerned started. Even if it was next year, I still had things I wanted to do. Marriage hadn't been on either of our minds until things had been pushed by both of our families. But at least his went about it in a little more decent way. His father hadn't drugged him in order to get Mike to the altar. His father, however; had paid mine off to stay far away from me. I could at least be thankful to my soon to be father-in-law for that small favor.

I hadn't heard from either my mother or father since that morning I'd woken up in Mike's... our bed. It helped that I'd been given a new cell phone with a brand new number that only the Cusumano's would have. Or anyone else that *I* chose to give the number to. So far, the only people outside of Mike, his father, or my new guard (and Mike's cousin) Giacomo had the number.

I'd spent all yesterday with Mike's female cousins Ilaria and Daniella, as well as his little sister Alessia preparing for today. Because brilliantly in my distraction, I had picked today to become his wife. It had been Alessia who found my dress while Ilaria and Daniella ooh'd and aah'd over the dress along with the flower selections. They each made sure that the flowers would work perfectly with my brand new dress and then we met with a hair and makeup artist that Daniella was very familiar with. Mike had given me a credit card that I could use without any limit the morning that I'd woken up at the estate. He'd wanted to ensure that I had anything and everything I could ever need. I'd never had anything like this before, but I was able to keep myself from blowing through it and possibly angering my husband-to-be.

Sitting up in our bed on our wedding day, I felt beside me to his side of the bed and realized that it was cold. He'd made it a point when we'd finally met that this was our room and our bed, that we would be sharing this bed every night from then on. Mike wasn't about to allow me to sleep in a bed without his body pressed against mine even after I'd made him promise that sex wouldn't happen until we were legally married. I hadn't hidden the fact that I wasn't a virgin from him, and he hadn't been phased by that which was a little surprising. But my mind was pulled away from remembering our first conversation about our marriage as the door was pushed open.

Ilaria and Daniella burst inside with both the hair and makeup artist that we'd hired the day before. Alessia wasn't far behind them as she bounced up onto the foot of the bed. I could tell that my sister-in-law-to-be was excited about today. I had a feeling that she was glad there would be another female in the house. She would finally have someone that she could talk with concerning female issues that wouldn't shy around the issue altogether like her brother and father obviously had.

Daniella hung my dress up on the back of the closet door and the women began to shoo me into the bathroom to start getting ready for the day. We only had a few hours and both artists wanted to have plenty of time to make me perfect for Mike. If only they understood, I didn't like being completely done up. I wanted to keep everything simple, yet tasteful. I would have been just as happy to show up at the courthouse this afternoon with Mike for our vows. But they'd both decided that I needed something a little more traditional as far as the ceremony was concerned. I wasn't privy to what they'd done, but I did know that Mike was involved in getting everything set up. I wouldn't see any of it though until I was walking down the aisle.

Chapter 7

Mike

The day was finally here. And surprisingly, I wasn't freaking out over the fact that I would no longer be a single man. There were plenty of extra hired staff on hand setting up for the intimate wedding that would be taking place within a few hours. I stood across the backyard in my tailored suit taking in what a few of our guys were putting together to make sure this day was everything that Carina and I hadn't planned for. I'd taken to the task presented to me by Ilaria and Daniella. They swore that Carina would be upset a few years down the road if she didn't get the actual wedding ceremony. They didn't seem to take into mind what my fiancé said continually. She had said she would be just fine with us heading to the courthouse, but as I looked over the arbor Giacomo and one of our other guards had built. It looked perfect. It wasn't too frou-frou and would look nice in the pictures that the women swore needed to be taken.

In less than an hour, Carina would walk down this aisle that the staff had put together. There were a few chairs setup on either side of the aisle constructed of white rose petals. In all honesty, Carina had already told me that she wasn't a virgin, and she knew that I wasn't one either. The white roses were supposed to symbolize purity according to one of the cousins, but that wasn't either of us. We weren't sharing that little tidbit with anyone because it just didn't matter. It wouldn't matter in the end; she'd be giving herself to me tonight either way.

A hand clasped down on my shoulder and gave a squeeze, but I didn't flinch. It was something my father had been doing for years. I took a bracing sip of bourbon from the rocks glass in my hand and gave him my attention. "The day is finally here, Michelangelo." My father said, looking over the part of our backyard that had been setup for the ceremony. It didn't matter how many people were there as long as Carina came downstairs. I knew she would, this deal worked for her as much as it did for me. But things were apparently moving faster than she'd originally anticipated. I couldn't help it that my hand on her thigh had been just the right distraction to get the date set. "I'm proud of you, my son. Carina truly is the perfect fit for our famiglia." Coming from Pop, that was high praise.

I'd witnessed for myself though just how Carina fit into our family. She was good for Alessia, giving my baby sister that feminine presence that she didn't get from the female staff members. She didn't take any of Pops' crap either, not that she was disrespectful, but she got her way with him almost as easily as she seemed to get it with me. She seemed to work a magic in this family that hadn't been there since my mothers' death all those years ago. She was a balm on my soul that I hadn't even realized that I needed. Sure, I still went about my daily business, doing things in my father's name that he couldn't or wouldn't trust to just anyone. But at night, I came home to Carina. And though we'd yet to consummate our relationship, she was still there every night in my bed and in my arms. Right where she belonged.

"Today, I don't lose a son. No, today I gain another beautiful daughter. And she is as beautiful as she is smart. Perhaps, she'll even get you reconsidering your own education, Michelangelo." I laughed softly and shook my head at the notion. Pop knew that school had never been my strong suit, but he'd always wanted a doctor or a lawyer in the family. It didn't help matters even now when I pointed out that he could still get that with Alessia. He swore that family business was a man's business only. He never wanted to put Alessia in that kind of position and I couldn't really blame him. I wanted to protect Carina from it as much as possible as well. "Now hopefully, you and your lovely bride will start working on making me a Nonno?" he asked.

He'd been harping on grandchildren for as long as I could remember. But I had to continually remind him that I was only twenty-two years old, and that Alessia was nowhere near old enough for a husband let alone a boyfriend. If he wanted those grandchildren, he was going to have to be as patient as I have been with Carina. It wouldn't stop me from trying to put a baby in her belly though. She knew that I was very anxious about us having sex before the night was over with. I'd gone long enough and her selecting today, whether she'd meant to or not, as our wedding day sealed it. "No promises, Pop. But we'll see what we can do to make that happen for you."

Chapter 8

Carina

The wedding had gone off perfectly. There was no one to object to our union, the cousins were seated behind us teary eyed, and then had come the kiss. The ceremony was beautiful, and I had been truly surprised with the arbor that had been put together. I hadn't missed the symbolism behind the white rose aisle, but I kept my mouth shut. No need to share my private life with anyone whether they were family or not. Mike knew my truth and that was what really mattered. Sure, Mike and I had shared a few kisses here and there while we'd gotten to know one another, but this… This was beyond words. I felt it all the way to my soul. My fingers gripped at the back of his suit coat collar to pull him closer. There were whistles, cat calls, and even clapping from his family as I held onto my husband for dear life.

We broke apart and looked into one another's eyes. I just couldn't pull my gaze from his. We were each trying to get our breathing back under control, but we were already being ushered back up the aisle. Could I help it that I just wanted to be alone with him? Even if it were only for a few moments? But there would be time enough for that later this evening. We needed to spend these few hours celebrating with family.

Apparently, my husband felt the same as we made our way to the family dining room where a delicious spread had been put together by hired staff. His arm never once left from around my waist. It felt like he needed to be touching me in some way as much as I felt the need to touch him as well. We were just keeping it simple and not rushing into what we both knew would be coming soon enough. As Mike held my chair out for me, I smiled as I eased into it and his lips pressed to mine once more. More whistles followed, but they were less than the ones' we'd received for our first kiss as man and wife. But for now, the focus would be on the family and the celebration of our marriage. A marriage that neither of us had really wanted at first, but even after a week together, a marriage we seemed to want to explore. Looking over at the man as my husband, he took his seat and laughed at something Giacomo said to him. I couldn't stop myself from reaching for his hand under the table and linking our fingers together. He looked in my direction and gave my fingers a light squeeze, his eyes showing the promise of what was to come tonight.

Chapter 9

Mike

The reception had lasted for hours, but we'd received some lovely gifts from my cousins in attendance as well as Pop and Alessia. Pop was going to be sending us on a special trip for our honeymoon within the next few weeks, a little something that he claimed every newlywed couple needed. A trip to the family island back in Italy where we could truly explore our relationship as man and wife before we would come back to our new normal. Carina knew that I would continue working with the family and would one day move up the ranks as my father had. He was capo for his years of service to *the* family and one day, I would take over the reins. He would spend the next several years preparing me for the role. He'd also made sure that my wife knew he couldn't wait to become a grandfather, a hint of a blush quickly rising to her cheeks. I'd already warned her of this fact, but she played the perfect part of blushing bride for him all the same. I'd also made it no secret to her that tonight she would be mine in every sense of the word.

Now I sat waiting for her on the edge of our bed as she changed from her wedding dress. It hadn't mattered how many times I'd told Carina that I didn't need any sexy lingerie to get me in the mood for her, she still insisted on putting on the special piece that Ilaria and Daniella had convinced her to purchase the day before. She said she wanted to wear this one something that would make her feel sexy all for me. But it honestly didn't matter to me. I didn't need a piece of clothing to see just how truly beautiful and sexy my new wife could be. All I needed to do was look deep into her eyes and see her. She was beautiful to me no matter what. Unbuttoning my shirt, I began to work on releasing my cufflinks as the bathroom door finally swung open.

In what felt like hours, but was more like seconds, she made her appearance. Standing before me was an absolute goddess and it took everything in me to not allow my jaw to drop to the floor. "Bellissima…" I murmured, dropping one cufflink to the floor as I drew in a slow breath. And she was. Carina was beautiful beyond words and I had to remind myself to go slow for her. As she took a step into our bedroom, I took one towards her, closing the distance between us step by step. Once she was within arm's length, I reached out and pulled her body to mine, crushing our lips together in a searing kiss. She tasted of everything that I was not, innocence when I knew she'd already given that away, sweetness, and lightness. "You are… so beautiful…" I murmured once more against her lips, resting my forehead against hers.

I leaned down, scooping her up into my arms as she laughed softly, holding her firmly to my body as I moved towards the bed. Someone on the household staff had scattered pink and red rose petals on top of our comforter, and I laid her on top of them so that I could have a good look at my wife. My wife! It felt strange to even think the word, but here she was in the flesh. So very beautiful and so very mine. Shirking out of my shirt, I moved to climb over her on the bed. Even though I knew that I'd already told Carina she would become mine tonight, something inside of me told me to make this right for her. To not rush this moment and try to make it as special for her as possible. I'd never once thought like that before and it felt strange, but it still felt incredibly right to me.

My lips met hers once more in a slow dance that they had become increasingly used to over the past week. Her lips, butter soft as our tongues slowly teased one another. I couldn't keep my hands still. With one hand holding most of my weight off of her smaller body, the other trailed slowly down her side, brushing against the side of her breast and giving a gentle squeeze. Carina moaned into my mouth, and I couldn't fight the smile as I repeated the movement. "Tease…" she murmured against my lips, obviously enjoying the touch as much as I did. Her hands didn't stay still for long, one dipping down to work the button of my pants while the other remained tangled in the hair at the nape of my neck. I loved the feeling of her nails trailing through my hair, whatever it took to keep me close to her.

"You know I'm not used to being gentle…" It wasn't a question. I was telling her pointblank. But as I looked down into her eyes once more, I let her know without words that for her I was willing to try. My kisses broke from her lips, trailing lower and lower until I had slid off the far end of our bed. I smirked as I looked down at her, the way her hair was already mussed, and the top of her lingerie was askew and knew that there had never been another woman like her in my life. Licking my lips, I snagged an ankle and leaned in, pressing a gentle kiss to the inside of her ankle as I watched the way she squirmed slightly at the difference in my touch. I wanted to do right by Carina and make this as good for her as it was for me. My lips worked up from her ankle to the spot behind her knee and up her inner thigh as I felt her reaching down to tangle her fingers in my hair. I knew that she had ideas running in her mind, but I had ideas of my own. I winked up at her as I pushed the lingerie aside and tasted my wife, my woman for the very first time.

Epilogue

Carina

It's been four years since we were married and each new morning dawns better than the last. I can say without a doubt that I am as in love with Mike as ever. There's never a day we go to bed angry with one another or alone. Most nights, it's just the two of us naked and cuddled up to one another after we've made love for hours on end. But a lot of nights, like tonight, I find myself staring down at the most beautiful little creature that we created. Our sweet little lion of a man, Leonardo, properly named after his grandfather. He is the absolute best even as he climbs in between us in the middle of the night.

We'd pretty much made Leonardos' year when we told him that he was going to be a grandfather. He was overjoyed, ready to tell the entire world even though we'd only just found out ourselves. I had to do some fast talking in order to get him to keep this information to himself, at least for a little while and until I was further along in my pregnancy. And boy did he dote on me. He was sometimes worse than even Mike in trying to keep me off of my feet. It didn't matter to him. We could already tell that our firstborn, and all of our children to follow, would be incredibly spoiled by their Nonno. He wouldn't take no for an answer on that. Who was I to deny him the pleasure of giving his grandchildren what they wanted?

Tonight, as I watch both beats of my heart sleeping soundly, I can't help but to be awed at the way Leo is cuddling even closer to my stomach. The rounded bump of his little brother or sister resting against his chubby little cheek, he even has one small handle resting protectively over it. I glance up and catch Mike as his eyes blink open, smiling gently as he takes in the appearance of Leo between us. "Looks like someone else is just as protective over his little sister as I am." He murmured with that same smile that got me when we first met.

I smiled as I leaned carefully over our two year old son and pressed my lips to my husbands. "We're not telling your father yet. I think we need to keep a little something special for ourselves." Yes, we'd been married for four years, had a two year old and another child on the way. My plans had changed over those years, and I couldn't say that I was upset by that in any way. I was still going to school, studying early childhood education, and it might have been taking me longer than I would like. But I have this amazing family of mine and I couldn't ask for anything more. I would have to say that I'd done pretty good for a woman who'd ended up married to settle her parents debts.

Author

Ashlyn Bragg enjoys spending time with family and friends as well as playing video games in her free time. She loves reading romance in her spare time and seeing how each author works their craft.